Mayflower Surprise

by Polly Peterson
illustrated by Jeffrey Allon

Harcourt

Orlando   Boston   Dallas   Chicago   San Diego

Visit *The Learning Site!*

www.harcourtschool.com

Ben glanced over at his mom, who had dozed off in the seat next to him, then looked out the window and sighed. There was not much to see from an altitude of 35,000 feet with a cloud cover below. He reached under the seat in front of him and eased his homework folder out of his backpack.

This trip has something to do with my social studies assignment, he thought. That much is certain.

He located the assignment sheet and read it one more time.

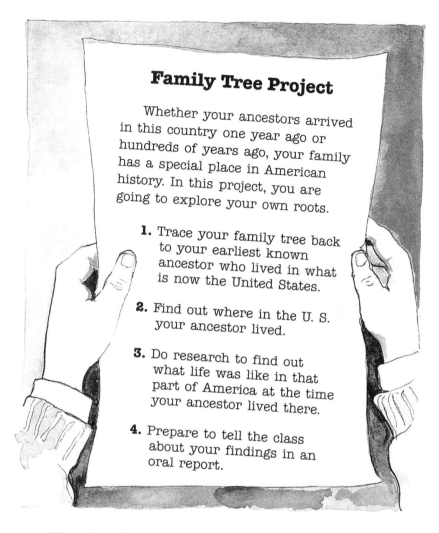

Family Tree Project

Whether your ancestors arrived in this country one year ago or hundreds of years ago, your family has a special place in American history. In this project, you are going to explore your own roots.

1. Trace your family tree back to your earliest known ancestor who lived in what is now the United States.

2. Find out where in the U. S. your ancestor lived.

3. Do research to find out what life was like in that part of America at the time your ancestor lived there.

4. Prepare to tell the class about your findings in an oral report.

Ever since Ben's mom had seen the assignment, she'd been acting very strangely, spending evenings and weekends on the Internet and dropping hints about some mysterious relatives "back east" in New England. Now they were flying across the country on Thanksgiving Day instead of driving to Uncle Raymond's in Tucson. How weird was that?

Ben stared out the window again, thinking about the vast distance between Arizona and Massachusetts. For Arizona's early pioneers, this journey would have taken weeks, even months, but Ben was traveling the entire distance in a few hours.

As they came in for a landing at Boston's Logan Airport, Ben finally had a view worth looking at. He pressed his face against the window to look at the boats in Boston Harbor. Choppy ocean waves were sparkling in the late afternoon sun. Could any place look less like Arizona? This trip might be a crazy idea, but at least it would provide an interesting change of scenery!

Ben was feeling excited when he got off the plane. To his surprise, there were no relatives at the airport to greet them. His mother rented a car, and they drove to their motel. Meeting the relatives would have to wait until tomorrow, she told him.

That evening, they walked along the shore under a starry sky. The air was clear and bitter cold, with a stiff breeze blowing in off the ocean.

"Just think," said Ben's mother, "the Pilgrims first landed in Massachusetts at this time of year. Can you imagine how they must have felt? On a night like this, they had nothing but their crowded and creaky old ship, their rumpled old clothes, and some stale, rotten food. There was no place to buy a meal, and no hope of a clean bed or a nice warm bath. The thought of going ashore must have seemed pretty terrifying, too. Who knew what dangers lurked in the unfamiliar land?"

For a moment Ben felt a little shiver of fear. He pulled his jacket tighter and looked behind him. He was almost disappointed to see street lights and houses instead of a dark, mysterious forest.

The next morning was sunny and cold as Ben's mom drove to their mystery destination. "It's almost time to meet the relatives," she said, "but you'll need to learn a little more about them first."

They followed signs to a place called Plimoth Plantation and pulled into the parking lot. "The first thing you need to understand is that these relatives of ours have never heard of us. For them, the year is 1627. We are part of a future that they know nothing about."

"Mom, you're not making any sense," said Ben. "Even the name of this place doesn't make sense to me. Isn't it spelled wrong?"

"Plimoth Plantation is a museum. The original settlement that the Pilgrims started in 1620 has been rebuilt here," explained Ben's mom as they walked toward the Visitor Center. "Back in the 1600s, spelling was much more flexible than it is now. You could write the same word several different ways, and no one would tell you that one spelling was right and the other was wrong. The people who named the museum didn't want this place to be confused with the modern town of Plymouth, so they chose an alternative spelling that the Pilgrims themselves often used."

"Okay, but what does this have to do with our relatives? Are you saying that we're related to the Pilgrims?" asked Ben.

"Exactly," said his mother. "I don't know if you remember that my father died when Uncle Raymond and I were very young. Grandpa Neil is actually our stepfather. Last summer, Ray decided to work on the family tree. He discovered that our father's mother was a *Mayflower* descendant. In other words, she could trace her family tree back to somebody who arrived on the *Mayflower* in 1620, and that means you and I can, too!"

Suddenly this crazy trip to Massachusetts began to make sense.

The orientation program at the Visitor Center helped Ben understand what his mother meant about "meeting the relatives." Plimoth Plantation was a living history museum. The Pilgrim settlement as it was in 1627 had been recreated as accurately as possible. Every detail, including the people who lived there at that time, had been included.

Ben's mother told him about their family tree as they headed for the Pilgrim village. Isaac Allerton and his second wife, Fear Brewster, were Ben's ancestors. That meant that Ben was related to both the Allertons and the Brewsters, two of the families whose houses had been reconstructed in the village.

As they walked past a sign telling them that they were now
entering the seventeenth century, the paved pathway ended. A
simple dirt track led them to a wooden fort. Ben ran up the
stairs and looked out. The view was fantastic! It truly looked
like another time. Little wooden houses with thatched roofs
were lined up along a dirt road that ran down the hill toward
the ocean. There were gardens behind the houses and farm ani-
mals in crude pens.

Men and women in old-fashioned clothes were going about
their daily tasks. These were the "interpreters"—actors who
had learned all about the food, clothing, activities, ideas, and
beliefs of the Pilgrims. Each interpreter had taken on the iden-
tity of a real person who had lived in the settlement in 1627.
They had even learned to speak the way people from England
would have spoken at that time.

Ben hurried down to the village and entered the first house he came to. As his eyes got used to the dim light, he saw a large black kettle suspended over a glowing fire in a stone hearth. A woman was bending over it, cooking something. Braided onions and bunches of herbs hung from the wooden beams overhead.

The woman was telling another visitor that six people lived in this house. Ben looked around in astonishment. The entire house was one small room. There was a hearth along one wall, a table in the middle, and along the opposite wall was one bed with a baby's cradle next to it. When Ben asked where the other people slept, the woman seemed rather surprised that anyone would wonder. The children slept on a straw-filled mattress on the floor, she explained, but for now, it was piled on top of a trunk in the corner. Above the hearth was another small loft for sleeping.

"Let's just hope no one snores," Ben whispered to his mom as they stumbled out into the bright sunshine and continued exploring the village. Ben was surprised to see a tall, bearded man in an emerald-colored wool suit with gold trim and shiny buttons. This person didn't look a bit like the Pilgrims Ben had seen in books.

"I thought you guys always wore black," Ben blurted out.

The man seemed positively astonished and wondered why anyone would think such a thing. Then he eyed Ben and told him that he ought to be wearing a hat.

"Protect your head to protect your wits," he advised. Ben felt himself turning red in the face.

Ben and his mom followed their map to the Allerton house. Ben dashed in excitedly, but no one was home. "Don't worry," said his mother. "We're sure to find some relatives soon."

They followed a path to a large brick oven that everyone in the village used for baking bread. A small circle of visitors had gathered around an interpreter who was perched under a tree nearby. Ben and his mom joined the group. A young Pilgrim woman sat on a bench answering people's questions while a baby girl played quietly at her feet.

The child was about twelve months old and was dressed like her mother in full skirts and a little cloth cap. When the baby began to fuss a bit, her mother lifted her to a standing position using strips of cloth that were sewn to the baby's dress—"leading strings" she called them. As the other visitors wandered away, Ben asked the young woman who she was.

"Fear Allerton," she replied.

Ben felt like shouting, Hey! I'm your relative!

Instead, Ben's mother began to speak. "We are delighted to meet you," she said. "Might we meet your husband, too?"

"He's not home at present," the young woman replied. "He's gone overseas to trade American furs for English goods. I married Isaac Allerton when I was quite young. My mother did not approve, but my father thought marriage would help to 'straighten my spine'."

Fear Allerton shook her head slowly and continued to explain, "I had been a wild, disobedient child. Living in Holland after my parents had gone to America only made me wilder. I arrived here in 1623 on a ship called the *Anne*. By then, Isaac Allerton's wife had died, leaving him with three young children to raise."

Finally, Ben asked the question that was burning in his mind. "Do your siblings have names as unusual as yours?"

"Yes," Fear grinned as she responded to Ben's question. "I have a sister named Patience and two brothers named Love and Wrestling."

Ben smiled as he imagined these strange and wonderful names huddled together in the top branches of his own family tree.

Later that day, Ben and his mother took a short drive into Plymouth to see the *Mayflower*. Ben was surprised at how jarring everything in the modern world seemed. He realized how much he was enjoying the sights, sounds, and smells of the seventeenth century.

He stopped briefly to look at a very ordinary-looking boulder that had been labeled "Plymouth Rock" and placed in a sort of shrine. Then he hurried onto the dock to see the Pilgrims' ship up close. The original *Mayflower* was long gone, of course, but the *Mayflower II* had been reconstructed to resemble the seventeenth-century ship as much as possible.

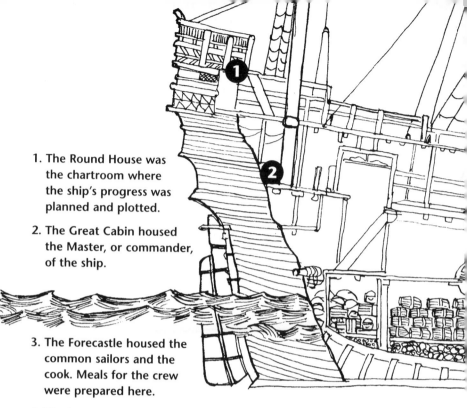

1. The Round House was the chartroom where the ship's progress was planned and plotted.

2. The Great Cabin housed the Master, or commander, of the ship.

3. The Forecastle housed the common sailors and the cook. Meals for the crew were prepared here.

4. The Lower Deck, or 'tween decks, was where the passengers made their cabins. *Mayflower* was not built to carry passengers.

5. The Hold was the main cargo space.

On board the ship, Ben located the cabins where the ship's Master and some of his mates slept. Apart from these few beds, there was no obvious place for sleeping. It was hard to imagine how 102 passengers and 20 crew members could possibly have squeezed themselves into the space. The houses in the Pilgrim village began to seem quite roomy in comparison!

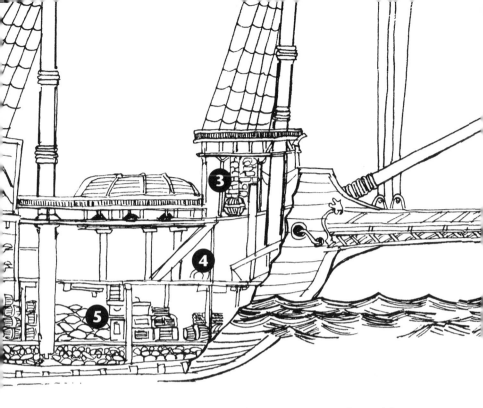

On board the ship, Ben struck up a conversation with an interpreter in modern clothes. He told Ben that he and a group of other young sailors had spent the summer working on the *Mayflower II*. They had learned how to set and furl the huge sails, how to steer the ship, and how to use old-fashioned methods of navigation.

Ben noticed a round platform high up on each of the ship's masts. "Do you ever climb up there to work?" he asked.

"Oh, yes," the man answered, "and much higher, too. Do you see those crossed sticks at the very top of the mast? On the original *Mayflower*, a boy about your age would have been sent up there as a lookout."

Ben had an urge to scramble up the rigging right then and there. He decided that someday he would definitely come back to Plymouth and learn to sail the *Mayflower II*. That would be a wonderful adventure.

For now, though, Ben was relishing the adventure he was having. Tomorrow, Ben and his mother were planning to go back to the Pilgrim village to find out more about their ancestors' lives, and they were even going to eat a seventeenth-century meal.

Ben gazed out and tried to imagine how it would have felt to sail across the sea hundreds of years ago. He noticed that his jacket smelled smoky, like the inside of a Pilgrim house, and the aroma pleased him. From now on, he thought, the smell of wood smoke would always bring back memories of the *Mayflower,* the Pilgrims, and his own surprising journey into the past.